# This Book Belongs to:

_____

_____

_____

_____

Rapunzel  Cassandra

Eugene

# My First Year
## as a
# Princess

studio fun INTERNATIONAL

# Our Story Begins

 Once upon a time . . .

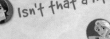 Isn't that a little cliché?

SHHH, EUGENE, I'M TELLING THE STORY THIS TIME!

ONCE UPON A TIME, there was a girl with magical golden hair, who was kept prisoner in a tower, far away from anyone or anything. It was all she'd ever known, because her mother had taught her that the outside world was a DANGEROUS, TERRIFYING PLACE.

But every year on her birthday, the girl saw mysterious, beautiful lights rise up in the sky, and knew—just knew—that there was a whole world waiting for her outside of the walls of her tower.

WANTED

Flynn Rider

One day, a thief—

A handsome thief.

Yes, yes, a handsome thief—broke into her tower, looking for a place to hide, and with a little . . . PERSUASION—

A FRYING PAN UPSIDE THE HEAD!

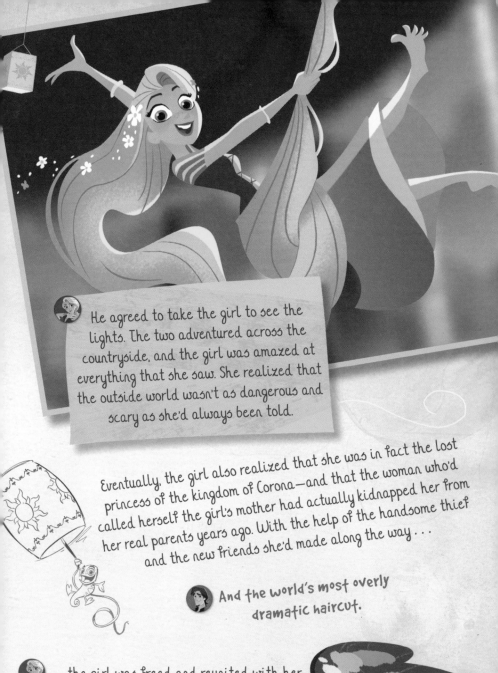

He agreed to take the girl to see the lights. The two adventured across the countryside, and the girl was amazed at everything that she saw. She realized that the outside world wasn't as dangerous and scary as she'd always been told.

Eventually, the girl also realized that she was in fact the lost princess of the kingdom of Corona—and that the woman who'd called herself the girl's mother had actually kidnapped her from her real parents years ago. With the help of the handsome thief and the new friends she'd made along the way . . .

And the world's most overly dramatic haircut.

. . . the girl was freed and reunited with her real parents, the king and queen of Corona. She and the thief fell in love, and they lived happily ever after.

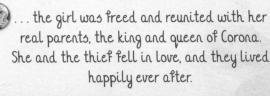

Or at least, that's how the stories usually go. As it turns out, though, real life doesn't like to give you neat and tidy endings like that.

Oh, I don't know, kiddo, I think we really landed on our feet. A castle, servants, my own on call manicurist . . .

# OH, DON'T GET ME WRONG!
Being back home in Corona and reunited with my mom and dad is great. But I'm definitely still getting used to the new normal.

Finding out who I really am turned out to be pretty complicated. The "princess" thing still feels completely unreal, and living your whole life in a tower doesn't exactly prepare you for running a whole kingdom, especially not one that you didn't even know existed until a few months ago!

I have eighteen years of catching up to do on history, geography, courtly duties . . . social skills and did I mention I'm (probably) going to be queen someday? Probably? Ugh, scary thought! No, not scary thought! It'll be fine! Don't get ahead of yourself, Rapunzel.

That's right, Raps. You've got this.

Cassandra and I might NOT agree on much, but we agree on that.

Thanks, Cass, Eugene. You're right, I've got this. For now, I should just focus on princess-ing. It seems like a good stepping-stone to um, queen-ing? Ruling? And I'll record everything I learn in this book. Writing things down has always helped me. It's kind of like talking to yourself, except it looks less crazy than when you do it out loud.

And we'll be right here to tell you when you're overreacting.

That's right. We'll be writing in this book, too, so you can look back and see how much we care about you, and to give you a little extra perspective on events.

Well, lucky for me, Corona is a wonderful place, and almost everyone I've met has been really patient and kind. For the sake of everyone living here, I want to become the best princess I can possibly be—so that
SOMEDAY I CAN ALSO BE THE BEST QUEEN I CAN POSSIBLY BE!

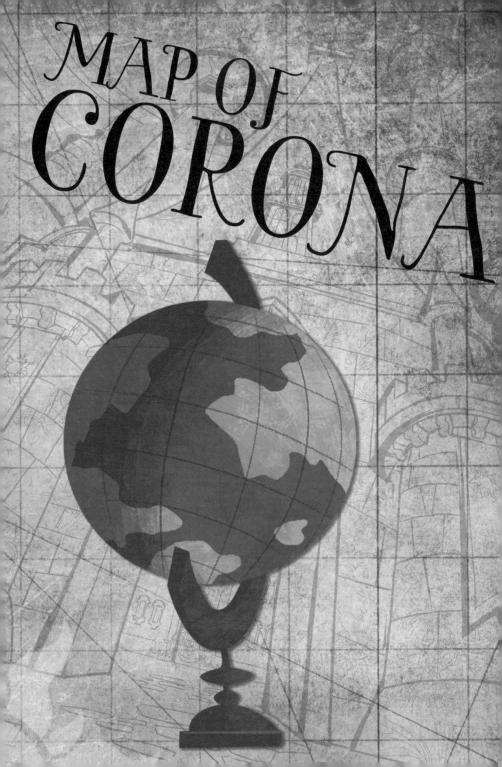

# MAP OF CORONA

# Corona Castle

In my relatively short time in Corona, I've learned a lot. One thing I've definitely discovered is that my parents can be really overprotective. Not that I blame them—having your daughter kidnapped from her crib doesn't exactly build trust in strangers.

MY DAD, KING FREDERIC, LOOKS PRETTY STERN. BUT UNDERNEATH THAT....

HE'S STILL VERY, VERY STERN.

EUGENE!

What? The man has a certain gravitas, it works for him.

He's actually very sweet once you get to know him. And I don't think I've ever heard my mom, Queen Arianna, have an unkind word for anyone. But sometimes they treat me as if I'm still the baby they remember.

I'm glad I have old friends who can help me navigate this stuff like you, Eugene—
**AND OF COURSE MAX AND PASCAL, TOO!**

 Always happy to help, kiddo. Eugene "helpful" Fitzherbert, that's what they used to call me.

I'm pretty sure they called you *"STOP, THIEF!"*

And new friends like Cassandra are really helping me adjust.

You have to have one friend who speaks English and isn't a kleptomaniac.

Hey, are you talking about little ol' me?

Yeah. I am.

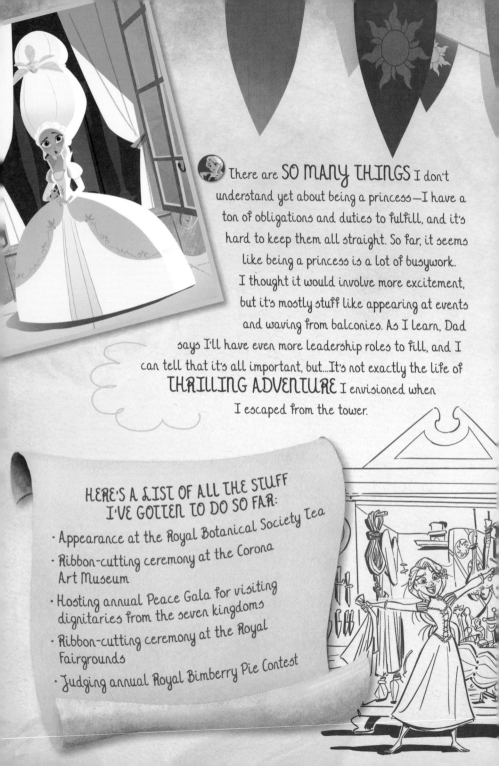

There are SO MANY THINGS I don't understand yet about being a princess—I have a ton of obligations and duties to fulfill, and it's hard to keep them all straight. So far, it seems like being a princess is a lot of busywork. I thought it would involve more excitement, but it's mostly stuff like appearing at events and waving from balconies. As I learn, Dad says I'll have even more leadership roles to fill, and I can tell that it's all important, but...It's not exactly the life of THRILLING ADVENTURE I envisioned when I escaped from the tower.

## HERE'S A LIST OF ALL THE STUFF I'VE GOTTEN TO DO SO FAR:

- Appearance at the Royal Botanical Society Tea
- Ribbon-cutting ceremony at the Corona Art Museum
- Hosting annual Peace Gala for visiting dignitaries from the seven kingdoms
- Ribbon-cutting ceremony at the Royal Fairgrounds
- Judging annual Royal Bimberry Pie Contest

Okay, that last one was fun. But what they all have in common is that they're mostly just about showing up. Being a figurehead is fine, but isn't a princess ALLOWED to get her hands dirty from time to time for the sake of her kingdom? When do I get to do something that REALLY MATTERS to the people of Corona?

**I THINK HAVING THEIR PRINCESS BACK IS WHAT REALLY MATTERS TO THEM.**

*Yeah, the rest of it might just take time and patience.*

Well, I'd be okay with that, but the worst part really is that my dad really hates it when I leave the castle grounds, which ... well, being STUCK in one place isn't exactly comfortable for me. You know, considering my history?

**ooh, yeah. Didn't think about that.**

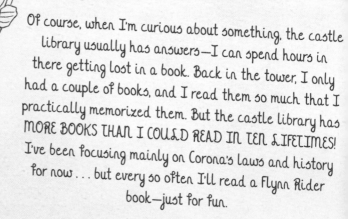

Of course, if you have to be stuck in one place, better a whole castle than just one tiny tower, right? I've learned a lot about my new home just from wandering around the castle grounds—and I've even figured out some really GREAT SPOTS to hang out in.

For example, my room is really a haven for me these days. My parents let me paint the walls however I wanted, which was pretty much the only thing that I liked about living in the tower. And in a place where I constantly feel like I'm being watched, it's nice to be able to find a little privacy now and then.

Of course, when I'm curious about something, the castle library usually has answers—I can spend hours in there getting lost in a book. Back in the tower, I only had a couple of books, and I read them so much that I practically memorized them. But the castle library has MORE BOOKS THAN I COULD READ IN TEN LIFETIMES! I've been focusing mainly on Corona's laws and history for now . . . but every so often I'll read a Flynn Rider book—just for fun.

## AWW! SWEETHEART!

I <u>love</u> to hang out in the stables, too. It's the best place to see Max, and no one is likely to bother me in there. And Max loves it when I hand-feed him some apple slices!

Why hang out in the dusty stables when the Royal Baths exist? I can't get enough of that place. I mean, endless spa treatments and footrubs whenever I want? Not to mention professional help in keeping my coiffure in tip-top shape—IT'S THE DREAM!

Ooh, people-watching is also super-fun. There's a balcony just off the north tower where you can see the whole castle courtyard. IT'S GREAT TO SIT UP THERE AND WATCH EVERYONE GO ABOUT THEIR DAY. What about you, Cass? What's your favorite place in the castle?

## The armory.

Dank, cold, and full of scary things. Just like you. Yeah, that checks out.

No need to be snippy just because I'm better with a sword than you, Fitzherbert.

Another good thing about having to stick close to the castle is that I've gotten to know everyone who lives and works here really well.

FOR INSTANCE, CASSANDRA'S DAD, THE CAPTAIN OF THE GUARD!

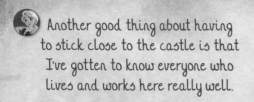

 It's my job to protect the citizens of Corona, and especially the royal family. I maintain security for the entire kingdom.

Yeah, you think King Fredric is grumpy? This guy is a total— totally amazing guy! So hardworking. Great mustache.

COG: Hmmm?

Oh, and Stan and Pete—they're guards, too, and best friends.

PETE

STAN

Absolutely. Couldn't do a shift without my best buddy!

How can you call yourself my buddy when you didn't even comment on my new haircut?

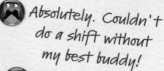

. . . You're wearing a helmet, Pete.

You should still be able to tell!

They do have a tendency to argue almost every second they're together, though.

Nigel is sort of my dad's right-hand man. He keeps track of schedules and royal duties, makes sure my dad is always where he needs to be, doing what he needs to do, and usually has good advice on just about every subject.

**Thank you, Princess. I do try to be well-versed in all subjects related to Corona and its history, in order to give the most prescient and relevant advice to your majesties.**

Kind of a stuffed shirt to be honest, but eh, it takes all kinds.

Don't forget Mrs. Crowley! She's the head housekeeper. I see her every day.

Ah yes, old "scowly crowley."

Hey, I got her to smile—once. She's really very nice once you get to know her and . . . leave her alone, and generally stay out of her way.

I don't want to be in your book. Shoo!

And then there's Freidborg, the Queen's lady-in-waiting.

Ah yes. Freidborg.

Right. Freidborg.

She certainly is . . . something!

SCOWLY CROWLY

Of course, no lady-in-waiting can hold a candle to Cassandra.

Yes, no one folds a tablecloth quite like our little Cassie here.

STUFF IT, Fitzherbert.

When I first got here I was completely in over my head. Everything was so new and so confusing! Cassandra was the one who was by my side all the time, showing me the ropes, teaching me everything I needed to know to get through the day, from putting on corsets to proper princess hand-waving techniques. SHE'S MY FIRST (AND BEST!) GIRLFRIEND.

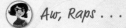 *Still haven't successfully gotten you to wear shoes, though.*

Shoes, shmoes. Really, lady-in-waiting is the least of what she does. As the daughter of the Captain of the Guard, Cassandra is a master of all kinds of weaponry and fighting styles. SHE'S A TRULY AWESOME WARRIOR.

*Thanks, Raps. I just wish my dad agreed with you. Not that I don't love hanging out with you—but I'd rather be on guard duty than laundry patrol.*

Oh no, I totally get it! I just hope when you become captain of the guard someday we still have time to talk. I don't know what I'd do without you, Cass. Our friendship may be new, but it already means the world to me.

*Aw, Raps . . .*

ARE THOSE TEARS? ARE YOU CRYING? GASP! RAPUNZEL, SHE'S HUMAN!

*STUFF IT, FITZHERBERT.*

# A New Mystery

... Okay, so update, Princess-ing is turning out to be more stressful than I thought. I really did. But then the royal coronation was going to happen and things just kind of SPUN OUT OF CONTROL.

*It might be kind of my fault, too.*

It just suddenly hit me that this ... the castle, the endless royal duties, Corona, all of this ... it's going to be my life. Forever. And I'm not sure I'm ready for it to be. At least, not yet.

*It probably didn't help that a certain someone decided to put even more pressure on you by proposing.*

**PROPOSING ON A NIGHT WHEN YOU WERE ALREADY STRESSED WAS NOT THE BEST IDEA, I DEFINITELY REALIZE THAT NOW.**

I JUST HAD TO GET OUT OF THE CASTLE FOR A NIGHT. BREATHE THE FRESH AIR AND CLEAR MY HEAD.

And since your lady-in-waiting also happens to know the quickest and quietest ways out of the castle, I took it upon myself to sneak you out. Which was dumb. But I could tell that you were about to start climbing the walls if I didn't.

Speaking of climbing the walls, Cass, you were awesome. You had all of the guards' patrol routes memorized, and you knew every back alley LIKE IT WAS THE BACK OF YOUR HAND!

...AND YOU HAVE THE CUTEST PET OWL!

HE'S NOT A PET. And he's not cute! He's intimidating. Anyway, knowing all that stuff is second nature to me. I sneak out all the time. You think my dad knows I'm out in the woods practicing archery and fencing and knife fighting and...well, you get the point. I have to do that stuff in secret. STOP MAKING THAT EXCITED STARRY-EYED FACE, RAPS. I KNOW YOU'RE DOING IT. IT'S EMBARRASSING.

 I CAN'T HELP IT, CASS! YOU ARE SO COOL.

Getting out of the castle really did help clear my head. It was nice to just kind of BE ON MY OWN with you and Max for a little while.

Yeah, well, I don't regret that part. But I probably shouldn't have brought you to see the black rocks. I just felt like you deserved to see them, since they were emanating from the place that the Sun Drop Flower used to grow.

YEAH, THAT WAS REALLY WEIRD. And then it was really weird when they started to glow when I got near them. And then I touched them.

And that's when stuff went down. The rocks started growing out of control—almost like they were chasing us. CHASING YOU.

We survived, thanks to you and Max, but not . . . um . . . unscathed. My hair—the seventy feet of magic, flowy-glowy golden locks that I thought was gone forever—had grown back.

 NOT A CONSEQUENCE I HAD ANTICIPATED.

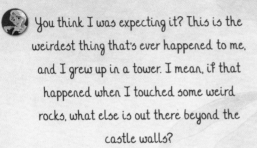 You think I was expecting it? This is the weirdest thing that's ever happened to me, and I grew up in a tower. I mean, if that happened when I touched some weird rocks, what else is out there beyond the castle walls?

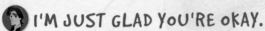 I'M JUST GLAD YOU'RE OKAY.
You were almost killed! I still can't believe you did something so risky without even telling me. I was turning the castle upside-down looking for you the whole time you were gone. I had to lie to your dad! I lied to the king!

# I'M STILL HAVING HEART PALPITATIONS.

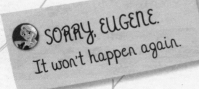 SORRY, EUGENE.
It won't happen again.

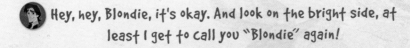 Hey, hey, Blondie, it's okay. And look on the bright side, at least I get to call you "Blondie" again!

## QUESTIONS ABOUT THE BLACK ROCKS:

- What are they?
- What are they made of?
- Where did they come from?
- Why are they unbreakable?
- Why did they glow when I got close to them??
- Why were they growing where the Sun Drop Flower grew???
- Did they make my hair grow back????

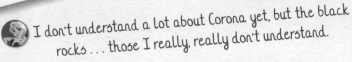

I don't understand a lot about Corona yet, but the black rocks . . . those I really, really don't understand.

I don't either. I found them by accident, and as far as I can tell, they only appeared recently—about a year ago, I think. AND I'VE NEVER SEEN THEM REACT TO ANYTHING LIKE THEY REACTED TO YOU.

MY DAD IS SO GOING TO KILL ME WHEN HE FINDS OUT.

Yeah, and if it gets out that I helped you sneak out of the castle, my dad is going to kill me. And then he'll send me to a convent for good measure.

YOUR SECRET IS SAFE WITH US, CASS. RIGHT, EUGENE?

Yeah, yeah.

# The Alchemist

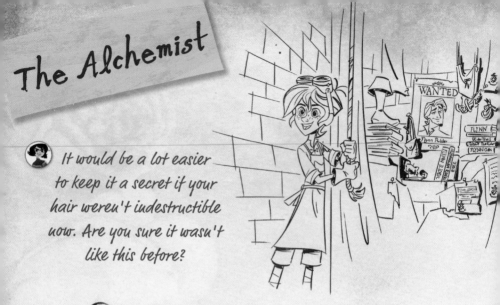

It would be a lot easier to keep it a secret if your hair weren't indestructible now. Are you sure it wasn't like this before?

NO! It used to be that if you cut it, my hair would just turn brown and normal and lose its power.

Yeah, I managed to slice it off with a knife. You remember—when I heroically died saving her?

Well, it's definitely not sliceable now.

That's why we went to see Varian, the alchemist. We thought maybe he could tell us more. And I kept having these really strange dreams all week. I think my hair was trying to tell me something.

WELL IT DEFINITELY WASN'T TELLING YOU TO SEE VARIAN. THAT KID WAS NO HELP AT ALL.

🗨️ I beg to differ! I managed to extract quite a lot of valuable data from the princess's hair thanks to the MIGHTY POWER OF ALCHEMY.

🗨️ Which we promptly lost because your other machines nearly blew us sky-high.

🗨️ Okay, that one's on me. But I still learned two very important pieces of data! One, the princess's hair no longer possesses its legendary healing abilities. And two, when the princess is in mortal peril, her hair acts to protect her.

I'm honored that you came to see me. And, don't worry, I won't rest until I've helped you uncover the secret of your hair, princess.

# Things That Can't ✄ Cut Rapunzel's Hair.

🗨️ THANKS, VARIAN. I'M GLAD I CAN COUNT ON YOU!

# All About Corona

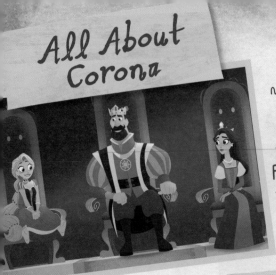

As it turns out, my parents are not super-jazzed about my hair coming back. Even though it doesn't have its magical healing powers anymore, Dad is sure I'm in danger again. He's FURIOUS that I snuck out, and he's forbidden me from talking about the black rocks to anyone, at all, ever.

WORSE, I'M NOW FORBIDDEN TO SET FOOT OUTSIDE OF CORONA'S WALLS WITHOUT HIS CONSENT.

Your dad has a point, though, Raps. Even if we spread the word that your hair doesn't heal people anymore, do you think anyone would believe it? He's right—THAT HAIR MAKES YOU A TARGET.

Yeah, but remember, locked in a tower for eighteen years? I'm not exactly a fan of the whole "You can't leave because I say so" thing.

I've gotta side with Blondie. She doesn't need anyone looking over her shoulder. I've seen her in action—**SHE CAN TAKE CARE OF HERSELF.** And if I'd been there with her—forget about it. I'd never have let anything happen to her.

I'm not saying she's not capable—you on the other hand . . . no comment. Still, you have to admit, Raps has a tendency to think the world is made of SUNSHINE-RAINBOW-PUPPIES.

Only sometimes! Eugene is right, I can take care of myself. (Also, I'm just saying, a world made of sunshine-rainbow-puppies would be amaaaazing.)

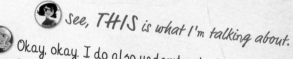
See, *THIS* is what I'm talking about.

Okay, okay. I do also understand why my parents are so afraid, and I don't want to make it harder on them. I just wish they trusted me.

I think it's the rest of the world they don't trust. Don't worry, Raps. **THEY'LL RELAX EVENTUALLY.**

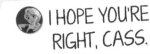
I HOPE YOU'RE RIGHT, CASS.

Not being able to leave Corona isn't so bad, I guess. There's lots of people and places inside the kingdom walls that I already know and love!

WELL... MOSTLY LOVE. I'M NOT A FAN OF MONTGOMERY. AND HE'S NOT A FAN OF ME.

oh yeah, Uncle Monty? Man, that guy is the best!

I'll admit, his sweets are delicious, even if he and I don't exactly see eye to eye on everything—or anything.

I run the village sweet shop, with recipes that have been handed down for generations upon generations. AND I DON'T NEED A NEW PRINCESS COMING IN TO TELL ME HOW TO RUN THINGS!

I still don't understand how the two nicest people in Corona don't get along. If there was a contest for "most likely to sing a song about kittens," I feel like you'd both be tied for first place.

WE JUST DON'T GET ALONG, OKAY? I mean, he really values tradition and I think . . . well, I think some things around Corona could change for the better. Changing the subject, how about that Feldspar guy, huh? What a cobbler, am I right?

Why thank you, your majesty! I do try to keep the citizens of Corona looking their best, feet-wise.

But Raps, how would you know? It's not like you wear shoes.

WELL, IF I DID, THEY WOULD DEFINITELY BE FROM FELDSPAR. And there's Xavier the blacksmith. Not only is he great at what he does, but he always has a story or legend about Corona to tell. He's practically the kingdom historian.

yeah, and he'll talk your ear off if you let him.

I merely try to impart the knowledge that I have gathered. And make horseshoes, fire pokers, swords— whatever the citizens need smithed.

And it's not just the people. There are many lovely places inside the walls. The bookstore is always great, especially if I'm looking for something that's not in the castle library.

Such as the latest Flynn Rider release.

They still make those things? PSHAW! LAME.

EXCUSE ME? FLYNN RIDER LAME? THOSE ARE FIGHTING WORDS!

NAME THE TIME AND THE PLACE.

You know what? Never mind. I keep forgetting that you are, objectively, terrifying.

There's also the fountain in the market square—even better for people-watching than the castle balconies. And I can always find people to chat with there.

When your dad doesn't send a cadre of bodyguards into town with you, that is.

Hey, he promised that wouldn't happen again. And the marketplace surrounding the fountain is a GREAT PLACE to shop. I can get paint and brushes, apples for Max, gifts for my friends . . .

A paper bag for Eugene's face . . .

And deprive Corona of the sight of my beautiful face? YOU MONSTER!

 WILL YOU GUYS PLEASE <u>STOP</u> FIGHTING?

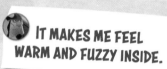 OF COURSE, I COULDN'T FORGET MY FRIENDS FROM THE SNUGGLY DUCKLING.
Vladimir is still collecting unicorns.

**IT MAKES ME FEEL WARM AND FUZZY INSIDE.**

 Big Nose is still looking for love.

 *The right girl is out there, even for a guy like me.*

 Shorty's still doing his thing.

 *And a very good evening to you, madame president!*

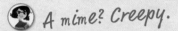 And so is Ulf.

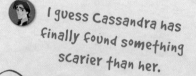 A mime? Creepy.

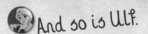 I guess Cassandra has finally found something scarier than her.

 Attila is working as the cook there now, and trying to open his own bakery in town.

**ATTILA THE BUN, COMING SOON!**

Hook-Hand is touring the world playing the piano, realizing his dream, too.

Good for him!

And his brother Hook-Foot has taken over his spot at the bar.

*WOULD YOU BELIEVE THE HOOKS ARE PURE COINCIDENCE? HAPPENED YEARS APART.*

Well, thanks to Cass, I made new friends in Old Corona, too. I'm so glad to know Varian, and I was glad to meet his dad, Quirin—even if it was under . . . less than optimal circumstances.

After the kid almost blew us all sky-high, you mean. Someone needs to have a talk with him about work safety.

Well, not EVERYTHING in Corona is safe. You're out in the real world now, Raps.

I know, Cassandra. I mean, there are more dangers out here than there were in my tower. I'm not saying that I don't understand my parents' concerns. I just want them to understand that I'M NOT A LITTLE GIRL WHO NEEDS TO BE PROTECTED.

But YOU ARE A PRINCESS, and like it or not, that puts a bullseye on your back. That's why you need guards like me to watch your back for you.

You mean ladies-in-waiting like you, right? Because you know you're not OFFICIALLY A GUARD.

**I WILL BE.** And then you're going to have to watch your back, because I'm going to—

Okay, okay, enough. Look, I know that the world isn't as perfect and safe as I'd like it to be. But it's also not as bad as you think it is, Cassandra. I'm living proof. I mean, if I'd judged the guys at the Snuggly Duckling by how they looked, I'd have gone right back into my tower.

Yeah, but we have a whole dungeon full of bad guys who are way worse than those goofballs.

CORONA'S MOST
WANTED

# Proving Ourselves

Okay, so one thing I've had to learn since I left the tower is that not <u>everyone</u> gets along all the time. Relationships were a lot easier when it was just me and Pascal. I didn't really have anyone else to talk to. But now that I'm out in the world, it's clear that when two people don't like each other, you can't force them to be friends. That sort of thing has to happen naturally, or it just won't happen at all.

Just look at me and Uncle Monty, for example. I did everything I could to try to become his friend, but in the end, our personalities were just too different.

I keep trying to tell you, Raps—being everyone's friend just isn't possible.

I should have learned my lesson from watching you and Eugene. EVEN LOCKING YOU GUYS IN THE DUNGEON TOGETHER FOR AN AFTERNOON DIDN'T GET YOU GUYS TO GET ALONG ANY BETTER.

Yeah, thanks for that, by the way. And hey, Eugene and I don't fight nearly as often as we used to.

Yeah, we're down to one argument per half hour.

BESIDES, IT'S NOT MY FAULT YOUR BOYFRIEND IS CORONA'S MOST WANTED.

<u>Formerly</u>, thank you very much. I've put my thieving ways behind me, thanks to Blondie here. It's the high road for me from here on out! Besides, you're the one who hides daggers in her boots and axes under her skirt. **I MEAN, WHERE IS THE WAR? SERIOUSLY!**

Don't tell me I make you nervous, Fitzherbert.

You know that you do!
Rapunzel, couldn't you have become bosom buddies with someone just a skosh less absolutely terrifying?

I worked hard to get where I am today. Unlike some people.

Well, one of us died heroically saving a kidnapped princess then magically came back to life . . . and it wasn't you. I'm just saying.

Still, as much as I hate to say it (and I really, really hate to say it), Cassandra has a point. I mean, as grateful as your parents were to have you back, Blondie, I still don't think they knew what to make of me.

Oh, Eugene, you're the love of my life, you know that. My parents know it, too. I WOULDN'T EVEN BE HERE IF IT WEREN'T FOR YOU.

Yeah, but I can't exactly make a living being your almost-fiancé. If you're going to be queen someday, then that means I'm going to be king, and no one wants a king whose resume reads "stole stuff, rescued a princess, then sat on his butt eating cake." I have to prove myself.

SADLY, THERE ISN'T A LOT OF WORK OUT THERE FOR A FORMER THIEF, PRINCESS-RESCUER OR NOT. I TRIED TO LAND A JOB AT JUST ABOUT EVERY ESTABLISHMENT IN CORONA. I tried to be a carriage driver.

But you couldn't slow down enough to listen to directions.

My way was faster! Then I tried being a cobbler. . .

**FELDSPAR FIRED YOU BECAUSE YOU'D ROBBED THE SHOP BEFORE.**

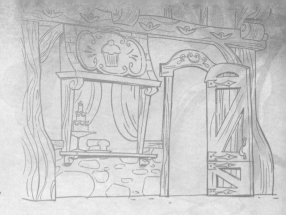

okay, I deserved that one. Then, I tried being a baker—

*And you almost burned down the bakery.*

If one pie bakes at 300 degrees, then 600 degrees should bake it twice as fast! The math checks out! finally, I was desperate enough to try out for the Royal Guard. It actually seemed like the perfect gig—noble purpose, snazzy uniform, and I'd get to protect Rapunzel. But your dad had it out for me from minute one.

*You're not exactly one to follow orders, Eugene.*

which is actually what makes me great at my current job. Training the guards how to think like a criminal.

*Think like a thief to catch a thief. I do have to admit, it's perfect for you.*

I understand the URGE to prove yourself, though. I'm going to be captain of the guard someday, just like my dad. Or at least, that's the goal. My dad's always been a little reluctant to give me the chance to show him that I'm qualified, so when he does, I have to be EXTRA READY. He won't give me the job if I'm just "good enough."

# I HAVE TO BE BETTER THAN THE BEST.

That's part of the reason I signed up for the Challenge of the Brave. Going head to head with fearsome warriors from all across the Seven Kingdoms and beyond! Surely that'll be enough to prove to my dad—to everyone—that I'm more capable than they think.

Besides, it's one of the few Corona traditions that doesn't involve cutesy-wootsey celebrations of love and friendship.

THOSE CELEBRATIONS ARE THE BEST PART OF CORONA!

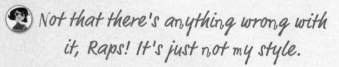

Not that there's anything wrong with it, Raps! It's just not my style.

I know, Cass. And I have to admit, watching you gear up for the competition was so EXCITING! That's why I wanted to sign up, too—so we could be amazing together. It didn't occur to me that I'd be stealing your spotlight.

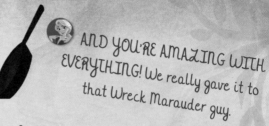

Still, it turned out to be a good bonding experience for us, Raps. I gotta admit, you are very handy with a frying pan.

AND YOU'RE AMAZING WITH EVERYTHING! We really gave it to that Wreck Marauder guy.

But you know . . . if you ever feel like I'm stepping on your toes, just tell me. I admire you so much, and you know I'd never do anything to hurt you, Cass.

I do, Raps. It's okay. I need to learn to express my feelings more, I guess.

YES, CASSANDRA. USE YOUR WORDS.

CRAM IT.

 fair enough.

# The Exposition of Sciences

EXPOSITION of SCIENCES

Brawn isn't the only thing valued in Corona, fortunately—it's also a place of great learning! I got my chance to shine at Corona's Exposition of Sciences. Or at least, that was what I was hoping for when it was announced. FINALLY—MY CHANCE TO PROVE THE SUPERIORITY OF ALCHEMY! But the competition was all flash and no substance.

Totally, Varian. The judge was utterly biased against *real* science.

You came up with like six inventions in one afternoon, Blondie. I think you did okay. It's not your fault most of them had been invented before. How were you supposed to know the yo-yo was already a thing?

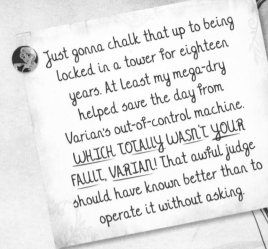

Just gonna chalk that up to being locked in a tower for eighteen years. At least my mega-dry helped save the day from Varian's out-of-control machine. WHICH TOTALLY WASN'T YOUR FAULT, VARIAN! That awful judge should have known better than to operate it without asking.

It's okay. There's always next year, I guess. I'm just glad you guys were there to help, it would have been a disaster otherwise! An even bigger disaster, I mean.

Is it just me or does Corona have a lot of celebrations?

Yes.

Because I love it.

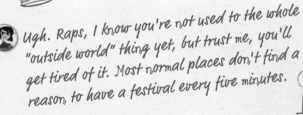 Ugh. Raps, I know you're not used to the whole "outside world" thing yet, but trust me, you'll get tired of it. Most normal places don't find a reason to have a festival every five minutes.

I dunno, Cass, I have almost two decades of catching up on celebrations, too. It's gonna take a while for me to get tired of all the festivities.

# Princess Practice

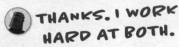 Maybe I'm speaking too soon, but I'm really starting to feel like I'm getting the hang of this princess thing. I mean, I think I'm still a far cry from being able to rule the kingdom on my own, but I did finally manage to do something other than just be a pretty face. You see, my old friend Attila was finally realizing his dream of opening a bakery. (Attila the Bun! Isn't that just the cutest name?)

That guy is so talented. Terrifying, but talented.

**THANKS. I WORK HARD AT BOTH.**

But then he was accused of wrecking Uncle Monty's Sweet Shop. Everyone was against him—including the captain of the guard and my dad. THEY WERE READY TO EXILE HIM!

 AND I WAS READY TO ACCEPT MY FATE. FOR A WHILE IT SEEMED LIKE A GUY LIKE ME COULD JUST NEVER MAKE HIS DREAMS COME TRUE ... NOT WHEN THE WORLD'S AGAINST HIM.

EVERYONE DESERVES A DREAM. And I knew that you didn't do what you were accused of—even though you look scary, I know you're so sensitive that you'd never really hurt anyone. You'd definitely never wreck someone's shop. I just couldn't get anyone to believe me.

I believed you!     ME TOO! I mean, eventually.

 THANKS, GUYS.

But my study of obscure Corona laws finally paid off! I was able to buy twenty-four hours to look for evidence, and even though it was a close call—a very close call—I proved that Attila was completely innocent.

Yeah, turns out Shorty and his goat were responsible for all the mayhem. Never did trust that goat.

What exactly is Shorty's deal, anyway?

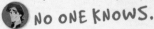 NO ONE KNOWS.

The important thing is, my parents saw that I'm capable of doing more than just being a figurehead. I can do things that matter for the kingdom! Oooh, I'm so pumped!

To be fair, your dad isn't <u>EXACTLY</u> the level-headed, King Perfect he pretends to be. At least, not all the time. Remember the prank war with the kingdom of Equis?

Oh yeah! You never did tell me the whole story.

### OHH, THIS IS GOOD.

So your dad has this life-long rivalry with the kingdom next door, and its ruler, King Trevor. Trevor pranked your dad by giving his statue an . . . UNFLATTERING MAKEOVER.

Ooh, I remember that! That was the day that Cass had to teach me what a prank was.

### *YOU GOT THE HANG OF IT. EVENTUALLY.*

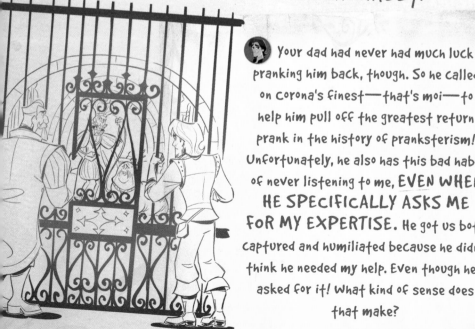

Your dad had never had much luck pranking him back, though. So he called on Corona's finest—that's moi—to help him pull off the greatest return prank in the history of pranksterism! Unfortunately, he also has this bad habit of never listening to me, <u>EVEN WHEN</u> **HE SPECIFICALLY ASKS ME FOR MY EXPERTISE.** He got us both captured and humiliated because he didn't think he needed my help. Even though he'd asked for it! What kind of sense does that make?

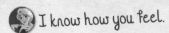 I know how you feel.

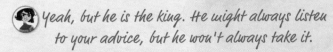 Yeah, but he is the king. He might always listen to your advice, but he won't always take it.

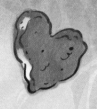

ANYWAY. He eventually admitted that he'd been wrong to ignore my guidance, and we worked together to steal the seal of Equis, which, by the way, was an actual living, breathing aquatic mammal and not a small signet ring or cylinder used to stamp official documents, which was very confusing.

I set it free in the Corona harbor, by the way. Poor thing didn't deserve a life with that jerky Trevor. And now your dad takes me seriously and listens to my advice!

MOSTLY. I MEAN . . .
SOMETIMES.
ONCE OR TWICE.

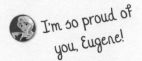 I'm so proud of you, Eugene!

# The Mystery Deepens

 **So . . . not-so-great news.**

The black rocks? The ones my father strictly <u>FORBADE ME</u> from talking about? They're inside Corona's walls now.

And I've figured out that there's some kind of connection between the princess's hair and the black rocks' growth. What kind of connection I'm not sure, but it's definitely there. But it might be too late to do anything about it. The rocks are already wreaking havoc in my village. And my dad's not exactly being straight with your dad about what's going on. I don't know what his motivation is, but I'm really worried.

 **ME TOO, VARIAN. BUT WE'RE GOING TO FIGURE THIS OUT TOGETHER. I PROMISE.**

Agreed, Princess! With alchemy, anything is possible.

As soon as my parents get back from this vacation they've been planning, I'll have my dad talk to your dad. In the meantime, I'll turn over every rock, read every book, and talk to everyone in and out of town to find the answers we need! With or without my father's permission.

GREAT PLAN, Raps— except that you're going to be in charge while your parents are gone. I don't think you're going to have much time for investigation.

We can't afford to delay too long, though—who knows how much damage the rocks will do if they get much farther into the kingdom?

# Disaster Strikes

Apparently, proving Attila's innocence also proved to my dad that I was ready to run the kingdom on my own. I mean, not permanently, but just for a couple of days while he went on vacation with my mom. I spent a couple of weeks shadowing him really closely on his daily duties, and I have to admit, I really did think I could handle it. It all seemed... not simple, exactly, but doable.

I just had to be confident. Decisive. Fair. When my parents left, I WAS READY TO MAKE THEM PROUD!

But it all fell apart so quickly. I spent my first day mediating disputes and trying to fix problems—but every solution I tried just made things worse, or more complicated, or created a brand-new problem that I hadn't thought of.

No one was expecting you to pick it up overnight, Blondie. YOU DID YOUR BEST.

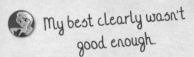 My best clearly wasn't good enough.

DON'T BE SO HARD ON YOURSELF, RAPS. I've been around royalty my whole life, and believe me, you've got the makings of a great queen. You just have to let yourself see it.

I haven't even started on the second day . . .

Okay, a GIANT snowstorm hitting Corona is definitely not your fault.

MAYBE NOT, BUT HOW I HANDLED IT DEFINITELY IS.

I mean, at first it seemed like just a normal snowfall. I mean, I'd never been outside when the snow was falling before! I was so excited that I declared a kingdom-wide snow day.

But it became clear pretty quickly that it wasn't an ordinary snowstorm.

Again, who would expect a snowstorm?

I should have, apparently. Then Max came back without my parents, and I thought they might be lost forever, and I had to send you and all my friends from the Snuggly Duckling out into the storm to rescue them . . . I was so scared, Eugene.

BLONDIE, IT'S ME. YOU KNOW I CAN TAKE CARE OF MYSELF. AND I NEVER TURN DOWN THE CHANCE TO BE A HERO.

Let me tell you, by the way, my rescue of the King and Queen was magnificently death-defying. There we were, on the crumbling cliff-face, your parents' overturned carriage on an outcropping below us. Lance and I used ropes and rappelled down toward them—only to be nearly undone by a sudden avalanche!

WE DUG OUR WAY OUT AND FOUND
YOUR PARENTS JUST IN TIME,
but the King was injured and in no
condition to climb. Thinking quickly,
I rigged a makeshift seat from one of the
carriage's wheels, and we used it to lift
the King to safety. It was a stroke of genius,
if I do say so myself. And we only almost died a
half-dozen times, if that. Really, it was nothing.

I appreciate you saving my parents, Eugene. But you know
the whole situation terrified me, right? While you were
gone I had to make the decision to evacuate the island,
even though I knew it didn't feel right.
I KNEW THERE WAS SOMETHING MORE
TO THE STORM.

Because Xavier told us that story about Zhan Tiri, right? That the snowstorm was a CURSE, and could only be dispersed by activating the legendary Demantius Device, deep under the castle.

RIGHT. AND WHAT QUEEN TRUSTS THE FATE OF HER KINGDOM TO A FAIRY TALE?

A good one. You were right—the Demantius Device was real, and you saved **EVERYONE**, Raps.

BUT I ALMOST GOT US KILLED! I ALMOST GOT PASCAL KILLED!

I had to send my true love into a deadly snowstorm, and I waited too long to evacuate the island, and Varian came to me for help. He was begging me to come with him to Old Corona, something was happening with the black rocks. Even though I'd promised to help him with those, I had to tell him that I couldn't help him. I had to turn down a friend in his hour of need. He got dragged off by the guards and I didn't even have time to say anything . . .

It was a state of emergency, Rapunzel. You had no choice.

I did have a choice. I just don't know if I made the right one.

**BUT YOU STOPPED THE STORM. YOU SAVED CORONA!**

But what if I'd been wrong? What if the device hadn't been real? What if we hadn't been able to activate it? WHAT IF—

**WHOA, BLONDIE. BREATHE.**

I hate to agree with Eugene on anything, but he's definitely right, Raps. You did your best in an impossible situation. You made good decisions.

DID I? I'M NOT SURE I KNOW ANYMORE.

RIGHT NOW, I'M NOT EVEN SURE THAT I WANT TO BE QUEEN.

# The Magic of Corona

Ever since the snowstorm, I've been feeling . . . not myself. I couldn't make decisions—even about little things. Every time I tried, I'd think about all the things that could go wrong, and I'd just . . . freeze.

GOOD ONE! Snowstorm, freeze! Sorry—too soon?

Kind of. I mean, I couldn't even paint something, and painting is my absolute, very favorite thing to do in the world.

Yeah, you without a brush in your hand is sort of like seeing Max walk on his hind legs. I mean, I've seen it, but I really don't know what to make of it.

And the problem only got worse when my dad tried to get me to paint a mural for the Gallery of the Seven Kingdoms. I mean, I'd been trying to get him to agree to open it for months. It was going to be a symbol of peace between Corona and its allies, and when he asked me to paint the mural for it, I was overjoyed! But then the what ifs started. WHAT IF IT WASN'T PERFECT? WHAT IF I PAINTED SOMETHING OFFENSIVE TO ONE OF THE OTHER KINGDOMS BY MISTAKE? WOULD I START A WAR? WHAT IF MY PAINTING WAS SO BAD THAT I BROKE UP THE ALLIANCE OF THE SEVEN KINGDOMS?!?

BLONDIE, DEEP BREATHS.

Jeez, Raps. I thought it was just painter's block—I didn't realize how much all the pressure was eating you up inside.

It's okay. I mean, it wasn't really about the painting. It was about . . . everything.

I guess that's why I was so willing to listen to Mrs. Sugarbee.

Yes, Mrs. Sugarbee, the evil demon who was secretly planning to release the ancient evil warlock Zhan Tiri onto Corona by painting a really, really ugly tree. IS IT JUST ME, OR ARE OUR OPPONENTS GETTING WEIRDER? Still, I should have known something was seriously wrong when your paintings got so unimaginative. THEY WERE COMPLETELY LACKING THAT USUAL RAPUNZEL RAZZLE-DAZZLE!
But I guess I was hoping that maybe you were just finding your artistic feet again, so to speak.

And I was busy investigating the mysterious disappearances of half a dozen Corona citizens. It was the first real assignment my dad had given me in forever, and I was so ready to make him proud. I guess neither of us was paying as much attention to you as we could have been.

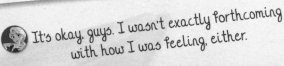

It's okay, guys. I wasn't exactly forthcoming with how I was feeling, either.

I'm just lucky that the disappearances turned out to be connected—and that Eugene made himself USEFUL for once.

I helped you solve the case, Cass, credit where credit is due.

UGH, FINE. I GUESS YOU WERE PRETTY HELPFUL.

It took both of us and Rapunzel to banish Sugarbee back to the netherworld with her boss.

I've definitely learned that Corona is a much more MAGICAL place than I thought. And I mean that literally.

Says the girl with magically indestructible hair.

Well, the Sun Drop Flower is just one of the legends of Corona that just happens to be true—I didn't know that there were so many more! And not all of them are so fantastical.

For instance, there's the Book of Herz Der Sonne, the centerpiece of Corona's Day of Hearts celebration. The king of Corona and the general of Saporia fell in love because of it, and now every year, those who have found true love can add their names to the book's pages.

It also has maps to secret underground tunnels underneath Corona. Wish I'd known about that during my thieving days.

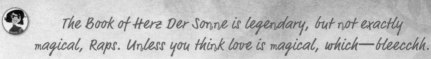 The Book of Herz Der Sonne is legendary, but not exactly magical, Raps. Unless you think love is magical, which—bleecchh.

I dunno, the book got you a date. Sure, the guy turned out to be a Saporian Separatist who was just trying to steal the book and start an invasion, but getting you to act all romantic for even one night is a bona-fide **MIRACLE** in my eyes.

WE ARE _NEVER_ SPEAKING OF THAT NIGHT AGAIN.

Okay, what about the engineer Demanitus and the Demanitus Device? You saw that with your own eyes, Cass. A giant machine underneath Corona that can control the wind! I mean, yeah, we kiiiind of broke it . . .

Was that magic, though? I feel like if Varian were here, he'd call that science.

You might be right. I wish he was here—he'd probably also be able to tell us more about the black rocks, too. But I haven't seen him since the snowstorm. I hope he can forgive me for not being able to help him.

## WHAT ABOUT THAT CREEPY ZHAN TIRI LEGEND?

Can we call it a legend when we came face-to-face with the evil warlock himself? Or at least one of his minions?

Right! Zhan Tiri was that evil warlock who hated Corona so much that he tried to freeze it in an endless snowstorm.

YEP, remember that. Lived it, in fact. His curse was what supposedly came back and struck Corona while your parents were gone.

Yeah. "When the kingdom was at its weakest . . ." Guess that meant me.

Some all-powerful evil warlock. He totally underestimated you. And so did that CREEPY Sugarbee lady.

Sugarbee wasn't even her name. What did she call herself? Sugracha the Eternal?

THAT IS SOMEHOW AN EVEN WEIRDER NAME THAN SUGARBEE.

Somehow I doubt we've seen the last of Zhan Tiri, or his curses. I just hope I'm better prepared to deal with them next time.

Yeah, it is kind of CRAZY that you don't have to just worry about the usual rogues and scoundrels, but ancient evil spells and curses, too. Of course, I'm talking to the girl with the magic hair, so maybe I shouldn't be surprised.

Speaking of all these legends, I feel like I heard about most of them from Xavier.

The blacksmith guy? Yeah, you're right, Blondie. The creepy, magicaly ones especially. That guy really has a way of bringing down a room.

It does seem like he knows more than he lets on sometimes. I mean, he knows how to make potions too, doesn't he?

JUST PUTTING THIS OUT THERE . . . IS XAVIER A WIZARD? HE'S A WIZARD, ISN'T HE?

That's the weird thing. He isn't. I mean, not as long as I've known him. He's always just been Xavier the blacksmith, a guy who makes horseshoes and swords and will talk your ear off about Corona history if you let him.

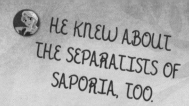 HE KNEW ABOUT
THE SEPARATISTS OF
SAPORIA, TOO.

 oh yeah, the ones that Cass's boyfriend
was working for.

For the last time, Andrew was NOT my boyfriend,
and if we bring this up again I'm going to throw
both of you in the lake.

I'M JUST SAYING, THERE MIGHT BE
MORE TO XAVIER THAN WE KNOW.

I've got to remember to ask him about the black
rocks, or I would, if my father hadn't forbidden
me from talking about them to anyone.

Yeah. Kind of
puts a damper on
investigation.

# Learning About Family

Okay, so one thing that's really wonderful about being back home with my parents is getting to know my mother and father as people. I mean, we were so OVERWHELMED by being back together at first that everything was kind of weird. My mom and dad kind of walked on eggshells around me for awhile, like they thought my return was a dream that they didn't want to wake up from. But now I know all kinds of stuff about them—like how my dad tells really bad dad jokes all the time, or how my mom used to lead an incredible life of adventure before she settled down and became queen.

## SHE DID? WHOA!

Yeah! After the coronation, she gave me a journal that she'd filled with all of the amazing stuff she did when she was younger. It's where I got the idea to start a journal and document my adventures!

My mom's sister, Aunt Willow, told me that when they were kids, her nickname used to be Dare-ianna, because she'd do anything you DARED HER TO DO.

It's wonderful to get to know all this family that I didn't even know existed before—Aunt Willow had so many tales about trekking across the world, climbing far-off mountains, and exploring forbidden jungles. Sometimes I wish I was living a life like hers.

But reading about my mom's adventures, and getting to spend time with her— that's a treasure I don't think I'd give that up for anything. And it's not like my mom has given up her adventuring ways completely. That night that we went to see the meteor shower with Aunt Willow, she ended up flying on a human-sized kite down a mountain! It was SO AMAZING.

But she's also an incredible queen and statesperson. I don't know if I'll ever be able to live up to her or my dad's legacy.

Trust me, kid. You're well on your way. My sister and brother-in-law have a lot to be proud of.

There you go getting down on yourself again, Blondie. IF THERE'S ONE THING I KNOW ABOUT THE WOMAN I LOVE, IT'S THAT SHE NEVER GIVES UP.

Yeah, Raps. Stop kicking yourself for not being perfect at something you're still new at. I MEAN, JUST LOOK AT HOW YOU HANDLED YOURSELF WHEN THE GRIFFIN OF PITTSFORD CAME TO VISIT.

BUT ALMOST EVERYTHING WENT WRONG THAT DAY!

only because of that wacky purple emotion potion. Reversing our personalities wasn't exactly helpful.

Pascal and Max were just trying to help. It was our fault for arguing so much.

*Things started off rocky, for sure. But once the potion's effect was reversed, YOU STOPPED YOUR DAD FROM DECLARING WAR ON PITTSFORD! I saw you put yourself between the Griffin and the King with a sword pointed right at you. Your selfless act snapped your dad out of his own daze.*

# YOU'RE AMAZING, RAPS.

We're not saying there weren't some speedbumps, Blondie. But you've got a way of handling things that always seems to make the situation better than when you started.

*Yeah, in your own Rapunzel-y way. So it's not the way your parents would do things—so what? You're your own person. You handle things differently.*

Aww, guys . . . you're going to make me cry.

🟢 I'm so LUCKY to have friends like you backing me up when I start to doubt myself.

🟣 *No prob, Raps. What are best friends for?*

🟢 Well, you guys are definitely my best human friends. But you guys know that my best-best friend is Pascal.

🔵 I can't believe I still rate lower than a frog.

 EUGENE!

🔵 KIDDING, KIDDING. YOU KNOW THAT I KNOW THAT PASCAL IS YOUR OLDEST AND DEAREST FRIEND AND I'D NEVER DREAM OF COMING BETWEEN YOU TWO.

🟣 Yeah, when Pascal went missing a few weeks ago, you were downright scary, Raps. I've never seen you so upset.

I couldn't help it! Pascal really is my oldest friend—he came to my tower when I was still just a little kid, and he was a teeny-tiny adorable baby chameleon. We grew up together, and he was the only one who kept me company while Gothel was away. Which was most of the time.

I don't think I could have survived the isolation in the tower if I didn't have him. And since I left the tower, I've come so close to losing him so many times . . . If anything happened to him, my heart would just break. I don't want him to ever doubt our friendship, not ever.

AWWW, PASCAL! I LOVE YOU TOO.

MY DAD HAS BEEN TIGHTENING SECURITY ON ME LATELY FOR SOME REASON. I only found out when I went walking and noticed guards practically shadowing my every move. You know, Eugene, you should tell them that they really aren't very good at being inconspicuous.

**YEAH, WE'RE WORKING ON THAT.**

I managed to sneak out to the Snuggly Duckling at least, but the captain of the guards was able to follow me somehow. Maybe not the GREATEST idea, though, since he ended up moving a club that turned out to be cursed and unleashing the vengeful spirit of the pub's proprietor.

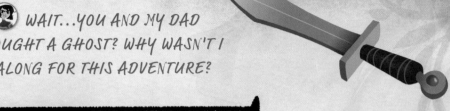

WAIT...YOU AND MY DAD FOUGHT A GHOST? WHY WASN'T I ALONG FOR THIS ADVENTURE?

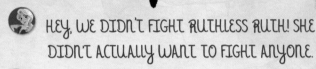

HEY, WE DIDN'T FIGHT RUTHLESS RUTH! SHE DIDN'T ACTUALLY WANT TO FIGHT ANYONE.

Hang on, the Ruthless Ruth? One of the roughest, toughest fighters in Corona history? And she didn't want to fight?

Nope, she just wanted someone to sing a song she'd written. It was a great song, too! Very catchy.

Figures. Only you could meet a great warrior ghost and discover that she was secretly a big soppy softy.

Well, I mean, she did trap us in some kind of otherworldly ghost dimension and threaten to kill us all by dawn if we didn't sing the song for her.

Now that's more like it.

THAT'S MY GIRL, LAYING SPIRITS TO REST WITH A SONG.

I did put her to rest, but she had some pretty important parting words for me. She told me that I couldn't wait for other people to make my dreams come true. I had to do it myself.

I dunno, Blondie, I'm kind of hoping some of your dreams don't come true. At least not the ones that you've been having lately, y'know, WHERE YOUR HAIR GOES NUTS AND TRIES TO FLING YOU OFF A BALCONY?

Those aren't dreams. Those are NIGHTMARES. Or maybe visions? And they've been getting worse lately.

I keep seeing the black rocks, and my dad, telling me to stay with him, and Varian is there calling for my help, but it's all confusing and strange. I feel like they're trying to tell me something, some kind of message. I just don't know what.

I know your dad told you not to talk about the black rocks again, but I think this is something you need to talk to him about. He's the king—he has to have some answers.

Believe me, Cass, I'm going to talk to him as soon as I get the chance. It feels like it's all building to something, and I don't quite know what it is, but I know that it's not right.

WE STILL HAVEN'T FIGURED OUT WHAT'S GOING ON WITH THOSE ROCKS, and I haven't heard from Varian in so long. I feel like he'll never forgive me for not helping him during the snowstorm.

DON'T WORRY. THE KID WILL COME AROUND AT SOME POINT.

YEAH, HE WOULDN'T LEAVE AN ALCHEMICAL MYSTERY UNSOLVED.

I just hope I can get him to help me before the rocks do anything awful. Last I heard, they were wreaking havoc in Old Corona—but in all the confusion after the storm, I haven't had time to look into it. WE HAVE TO PUT AN END TO THIS BEFORE ANYONE GETS HURT.

## Our Story Begins

I CAN'T BELIEVE IT. I JUST CAN'T BELIEVE IT.

It's okay, Blondie. You don't have to write anything down right now.

No, I have to get it all down while I can remember it in detail.

I FINALLY HEARD FROM VARIAN. He sent me a letter, telling me that he needed my help more than ever before. He said he'd found the key to the black rocks, and asked me to fetch a cask from his lab in Old Corona. Of course, I'd do anything to help Varian, so I left right away to do what he asked.

WHAT WE FOUND WAS SO HORRIBLE... Old Corona had been almost entirely covered by the black rocks! I was so confused, because I'd talked to my dad earlier, and he'd promised me that the black rocks had been removed, and everyone in Old Corona was fine.
BUT EVERYTHING WAS NOT FINE.

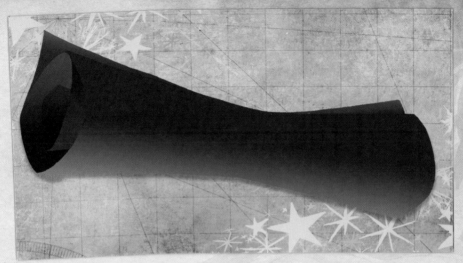

When we went into Varian's lab, we found Varian's father, Quirin, encased in the rocks. Frozen. I finally understood why Varian had been so frantic the night of the storm, and I was even more determined to help him. Luckily, we'd recovered the cask that he asked us to get for him.

Unfortunately, a bunch of creeps in black cloaks and masks were hot on our tail, and wanted to steal the cask from us—or should I say, the scroll, since that was what was hidden inside.

We managed to shake them for a while by hiding out in Rapunzel's old tower, but it didn't keep them off the trail for long.

YEAH, AND IN THE PROCESS OF ESCAPING, WE SORT OF DESTROYED THE TOWER.

I DESTROYED IT.

I'm sorry, Blondie. I know that place held a lot of memories for you.

Yeah. . .I spent my entire life in that place. I still don't know how to feel about it being gone. A little relieved and a little sad, I guess.

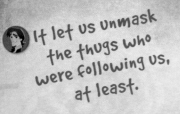 It let us unmask the thugs who were following us, at least.

Who turned out to be my dad and the rest of Corona's Royal Guards.

Which is how I found out my dad had been lying to me for months. I thought maybe he just didn't know that the rocks had gotten as bad as they had—but he'd known all along.

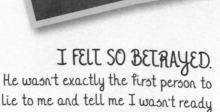

**I FELT SO BETRAYED.** He wasn't exactly the first person to lie to me and tell me I wasn't ready for the real world.

I went back to the castle to confront my father, but he didn't have any plans or answers. I just didn't understand how he could be so complacent—our kingdom was in danger and it was like I was the only one who wanted to do something about it! Of course, I didn't know what I could do ...

But Varian did. He found me, told me he'd managed to translate the scroll that I'd recovered, and that the black rocks were some kind of ancient warning of a **TERRIBLE** darkness—a darkness that could only be stopped with the power of the Sun Drop Flower.

My dad had told me the flower was long gone, but as Varian pointed out, my father hasn't exactly been a reliable source of information. He convinced me that for the good of Corona, we had to break into the royal vault and steal the flower.

I knew our best bet was to use Herz Der Sonne's journal and its complete map of the kingdom tunnels to get past the vault's security . . . so I stole that, too.

Is it wrong that I'm a teensy bit proud of you?
## BREAKING RULES, STEALING STUFF . . .

*Committing treason?*
*Not the time, Eugene.*

Not that Cassandra and I were twiddling our thumbs while you and Varian were doing your thing. **THE CASTLE WAS IN TOTAL TURMOIL.** Everyone was saying whatever was on their minds, like they were under the influence of some kind of truth serum. Everyone was crying, arguing, fighting.

Eventually we figured out that someone had given every inhabitant of the castle cookies laced with a modified version of Xavier's mood potion.

And that someone was Varian. He'd used it to find out where the Sun Drop Flower was hidden, and create enough of a distraction that no one would notice him stealing it.

All of which I figured out once we'd reached the vault . . . but I was too late. Varian had lied to me too—he never intended to use it to help Corona. He wanted to help his father, which I understood, but he'd put everyone in even greater danger to get it when he could have just asked for my help.

I thought I could trust Varian. I thought he was my friend. But he stole the flower and ran, and I . . .

IT'S OKAY, RAPS. NONE OF US COULD HAVE PREDICTED THIS . . .

Not that it seemed to matter. The flower must not have had what he needed, because he came back the next day. FOR ME.

He used some kind of machine to attack the castle. What was it? An automaton? We managed to stop it, but the king COMPLETELY FREAKED OUT.

He ordered me locked in my room in the tallest tower of the castle. For my own safety.

I still don't understand how King Frederic could think for a minute that was okay. HE WAS DOING EXACTLY WHAT GOTHEL DID! Not that the actual being locked up posed a problem, of course. It's not the first time I've helped you escape from a tower.

But this time you didn't do it alone. My dad was going to send me to a convent for sneaking you out of the castle at the coronation, but I wasn't going to stand for it.

All right, with some minor help from Cass and the Snuggly Duckling's cast of lovable rogues, WE MANAGED TO BUST BLONDIE OUT.

Just in time for Varian's next attack. This time he'd mutated his poor pet raccoon, Ruddiger, into some kind of hideous monster thing.

And he covered the whole kingdom in a thick fog so we couldn't see where he was coming from.

NOTHING WE COULDN'T HANDLE.

He took out half the castle's guards! Including your dad, Cass!

Cassandra's right. We absolutely had it handled. A little monster hide-and-seek isn't anything we couldn't deal with.

Unfortunately, that was Varian's plan all along. He'd never planned for Ruddiger to be anything but a distraction—he made it seem like his target was me. BUT HE WAS REALLY AFTER MY MOM. While we were busy fighting, he used the decreased security to kidnap her and take her back to Old Corona.

WE PLAYED RIGHT INTO HIS HANDS.

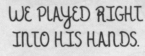

I TRIED TO CONVINCE MY DAD THAT WE COULDN'T JUST ATTACK VARIAN HEAD ON, BUT AT FIRST, HE WAS IN TOO MUCH PAIN TO LISTEN TO ME. AND HE TOLD ME SOMETHING IMPORTANT.

On the night he used the Sun Drop Flower to save my mother's life, he was given a warning— if he used its power, if he took the Flower's light for himself, he would unleash a terrible darkness on the land. Varian had been right about one thing—the Sun Drop Flower, my hair, the black rocks, they were all connected.

My father had known about the rocks all along, and had tried to ignore them, expecting everyone to do the same.

But he finally understood that they were destroying Corona and that it was his actions that had caused them to grow in the first place. He was ashamed that he'd put my mother and me above his kingdom. That was why he'd tried so hard to hide the truth. I managed to convince him that we could save Corona together—and together we came up with a plan to do it.

Varian was expecting an all-out attack on Old Corona, and we'd give him one, but my father and I would use the secret tunnels to sneak in the back way and hopefully free my mother before he knew what was happening. We united the citizens for the assault—Feldspar, Xavier, even old lady Crowley was willing to fight with us. We hoped if we kept him distracted, he might slip up.

Eugene and I led the assault, and for a little while there, I really thought it was going to work. But we'd underestimated Varian again. HE WAS READY FOR OUR ATTACK WITH HIS OWN ARMY OF AUTOMATONS.

WE WERE READY FOR HIM, TOO! Though not as ready as I would have liked. He did kick our butts for a while there.

And he ambushed my dad and me almost the moment we set foot inside his laboratory. He'd realized that the magic of the Sun Drop Flower was in my hair— and since it was as indestructible as the rocks, he wanted to try using my hair as a drill to shatter the rocks and free his father. To make his point, he threatened my mom with the same fate as his dad. I HAD TO DO WHAT HE ASKED.

It didn't work—instead my hair started sparking with magic and my body felt like it was going to shatter into pieces instead. I passed out, and when I woke up, my parents were trying to free me from Varian's machine.

I GUESS VARIAN COULDN'T ACCEPT THE FACT THAT HIS PLAN HAD FAILED. He appeared, piloting this giant piece of mechanical armor, and used it to attack me and my parents. We rushed outside to escape, but he was right behind us. He grabbed my mom and Cass, and the next thing I knew, the black rocks were bursting out of the ground, rushing toward me, and my hair was whipping around me like it had a mind of its own and then . . .

## I WAS CONTROLLING THE ROCKS!

It was like they were responding to my thoughts. I smashed Varian's army of robots and destroyed his mechanical armor. I felt powerful and strange and like every nerve was on fire, and then it just stopped.

And I stopped.
And I fainted.
And woke up in Eugene's arms.

I've got to say, I'm not in favor of this whole "almost dying" birthday tradition we've got going on. Next year let's just have cake. EVERYONE LIKES CAKE.

Seconded.

Varian was apprehended, and my father promised to get him the help he needed, and work tirelessly to free Quirin from his amber prison.

And the black rocks had burst through the outer walls of Corona, and formed a kind of road, leading far off into the distance. Whatever they were, wherever they were going, they were telling me to follow them.

Even my father agreed—and told me to follow my heart, and the path that the rocks were showing me. THEIR PURPOSE WASN'T TO DESTROY CORONA, BUT TO FIND ME, AND LEAD ME SOMEWHERE.

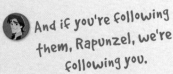 And if you're following them, Rapunzel, we're following you.

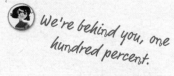 We're behind you, one hundred percent.

We still have to solve the mystery of the black rocks, the darkness, the Sun Drop Flower, my hair . . .

Those answers are out there, outside of Corona.

# AND WE'RE GOING TO FIND THEM TOGETHER!

**Studio Fun International**

An imprint of Printers Row Publishing Group

A division of Readerlink Distribution Services, LLC

10350 Barnes Canyon Road, Suite 100, San Diego, CA 92121 www.studiofun.com

Written by Rachel Upton

Designed by Tiffany Meador-LaFleur

Cover Design by Kara Kenna

ISBN: 978-0-7944-4107-4

Manufactured, printed, and assembled in Shaoguan, China. First printing, November 2017. SL/11/17

21 20 19 18 17 1 2 3 4 5